Disney's
POOH'S GRAND ADVENTURE
The Search For Christopher Robin

A

MOVIE STORYBOOK

Once upon the last day of a golden summer, Winnie the Pooh and his very best friend, Christopher Robin, shared many grand adventures in a remarkable place called the Hundred-Acre Wood. They chased each other through a meadow filled with butterflies. They played hide-and-seek in a maze of roses. And they sailed down the river on a raft just right for two.

As the sun went down and the fireflies began to blink, Christopher Robin gently told Pooh, "Promise me you'll always remember: You're braver than you believe, and stronger than you seem, and smarter than you think."

"Oh, that's easy," Pooh replied. "We're braver than a bee and taller than a goose…or was that a moose?"

"Silly old bear," laughed Christopher Robin. "Just remember that even if we're apart, I'll always be with you."

The next morning, Winnie the Pooh awoke to a brightly colored leaf tickling his nose. "It's autumn!" he cried.

As Pooh ambled outside to play in the leaves, he stumbled upon a honey pot. Pooh looked thoughtfully at the pot.

"I'll have to find Christopher Robin and ask him whose pot this is," Pooh decided.

Pooh found Piglet and Eeyore and Rabbit and Tigger, too.

But Christopher Robin was nowhere to be found.

"Why don't you check the note and find out whose it is?" asked Rabbit, pointing to the side of the pot.

"Oh," said Pooh, "there is a note, isn't there? I'd read it if I could—but...I can't. Perhaps we should find Owl."

"D-e-a-r..." Owl began, studying the note carefully. "This is from Christopher Robin," he announced. "Oh, dear. It says that he has gone to Skull, a most forbidden and faraway place."

"Then we must help him!" Pooh cried, and the others agreed. At once, Owl began to draw a map for Pooh and his friends to follow.

"This will be a long and dangerous journey," Owl warned. "You'll find Christopher Robin in the eye of the Skull itself."

And so Pooh, Piglet, Rabbit, Eeyore, and Tigger embarked upon their quest for Christopher Robin and soon entered a dark and prickly forest of thorns.

"You don't suppose," said Piglet, "that there are any h-h-heffalumps in here?"

"Of course not," said Rabbit. "The map says we're in a 'lovely meadow.' Ah, see? There's a golden dahlia daffodilius—"

Snap! went the huge plant, sending the reluctant adventurers running lickety-split toward a lighter place.

On the far side of the forest in a peaceful valley of flowers, a swarm of friendly butterflies lifted Piglet into the air. Piglet flew up so high he was too afraid to look down!

Then, by chance, his foot caught Pooh's shirt and lifted him into the air, too. One by one, the weary butterflies let go, and Pooh and Piglet landed softly back on the ground.

"Thank you, Pooh," said Piglet. "Saving me was very brave."

"You're brave, too, Piglet," replied Pooh. "Braver than—er—something. Christopher Robin told me, but I can't remember."

"We need to follow the map, map, map!" Rabbit explained to his friends. "If we follow our eyes, we'll get lost for sure!"

"But," said Pooh, "those mountains over there look just like…"

"No! No!" cried Rabbit, waving his hands in the air. Unfortunately, the map got caught on a branch and ripped in two, sending half of it blowing away in the wind!

"I got it," shouted Tigger. In his enthusiasm, Tigger bounced himself right onto a log overhanging a deep gorge, but he couldn't seem to bounce himself high enough to catch the map.

Pooh and the others tried to rescue Tigger; but the log cracked, and the friends dropped down into a squishy, muddy river.

After so many adventures, everyone needed to rest.

"I wasn't strong enough to get the map," sighed Tigger.

"And I wasn't smart enough to read it," said Rabbit glumly.

Meanwhile, a very lonely Pooh went out to sit by himself and look up at the sky. "Christopher Robin," he said aloud to his absent friend, "I've looked all the places you aren't. I just can't find the places you are. I really don't know where else to look." At last, the tired bear closed his eyes as Rabbit gently put a blanket over him.

A sunny day dawned, and the friends reached the dreaded Skull Cave at last. But once inside, they couldn't figure out how to get to the eye of the Skull to save Christopher Robin.

Suddenly, Rabbit had a very smart idea. But it required some strength from Tigger to bounce high enough to reach a ledge above them. And it required Piglet to be brave enough to climb onto the ledge and throw a vine down to the others so that they could climb up. Determined to do their best, the friends set to work.

"We d-did it?" said Piglet a little while later when they had all reached the top of the cave.

Just then a huge, dark shadow appeared…and it was creeping closer!

"Christopher Robin!" Piglet suddenly cried. "We came to rescue you from Skull!"

Later, Christopher Robin explained that he had left the note on Pooh's honey pot to let Pooh know that he was going to school—not Skull.

"Why do you have to go to school, anyway?" Pooh asked.

"To learn things," said Christopher Robin. "But remember, even if we're apart, I'll always be with you."

"And I'll always be with you," said Pooh, just happy to be with his very best friend.